D0815558

RISE OF THE TEENAGE MUTANT NINJA TURTLES

NINJA POWER

**Adapted by
David Lewman**

Random House New York

© 2018 Viacom International Inc. and Viacom Overseas Holdings C.V.
All rights reserved. Published in the United States by Random House
Children's Books, a division of Penguin Random House LLC,
1745 Broadway, New York, NY 10019, and in Canada by
Penguin Random House Canada Limited, Toronto. Random House and
the colophon are registered trademarks of Penguin Random House LLC.
Nickelodeon, Rise of the Teenage Mutant Ninja Turtles, and all related titles,
logos, and characters are trademarks of Viacom International Inc. and
Viacom Overseas Holdings C.V.
Based on characters created by Peter Laird and Kevin Eastman.
rhcbooks.com
ISBN 978-0-525-64503-0 (trade)—ISBN 978-0-525-70765-3 (lib. bdg.)
Printed in the United States of America
10 9 8 7 6 5 4 3 2 1

CONTENTS

MYSTIC MAYHEM

CHAPTER ONE

April O'Neil here! I've lived in New York City for all sixteen years of my life, and I've seen some amazing things.

Including four brothers who happen to be talking turtles.

I met them five years ago when they were sneaking around the basketball court on the roof of my apartment building. We became friends. Really good friends. They're like big brothers to me.

Except, you know, they're turtles.

Raphael is the biggest, oldest brother. We all call him Raph. They tell me he's a snapping turtle, but I've never seen him snap. Because he's the biggest and the oldest, he's the leader. But when you're fifteen, it's tough getting your brothers to follow you.

Leonardo's fourteen, and he's supposed to be the kind of turtle called a red-eared slider. Leo's really funny and cool. He makes me laugh all the time. He's also incredibly quick when he goes into fighting mode.

Donatello's also fourteen. He's a soft-shelled turtle, so he wears these amazing battle shells that he makes himself. He can make pretty much anything. Donnie's supersmart.

At thirteen, Michelangelo's the youngest brother. They say Mikey's a box turtle, but he doesn't seem very boxy to me. He's incredibly enthusiastic about all kinds of things, like break dancing, skateboarding, graffiti art, music, and basically running around being wild. He's really fun!

They all are! Along with their dad, Master Splinter, the Turtles were the weirdest things I'd ever seen in New York. Until we met Mayhem and found the Hidden City . . .

Listen up and I'll tell you about how we met Mayhem, why I named him that, and how he became my pet. Most of what happened I was there for, and the rest the guys filled me in on. . . .

Raph was the one who first spotted the strange little animal wandering around a construction site. When we got closer, we saw how odd the creature looked. He had a long tail, big pointy ears, huge eyes, and a couple of long teeth sticking out of his mouth. We couldn't tell whether he was a dog or a cat. Or something completely different!

Raph started talking to him like he was talking to a baby. "Hey, little guy," he cooed. "Whatcha doing here? Come to big Raphie. He'll make everything okay!"

His brothers just stared at him.

"What?" Raph asked. "Pets love me. I am one with the animals!"

But the animal jumped into MY arms! He licked MY face! I loved it!

"He looks so weird," Mikey said. "What is he?"

"A dog? A cat?" Leo said. "A rainbow weasel? Just made that up."

Donnie spotted a glowing pink vial on

the animal's collar. "Maybe he's some kind of nuclear Saint Bernard."

Before we could decide what he was, two dudes in jogging suits ran into the construction site. This was not cool. The Turtles can't let people see them, or else they might end up being dissected in some lab.

"Humans!" Raph hissed. "Plan H!"

Leo spoke to the joggers in a super-nerdy voice. "Excuse me, sirs. Can you direct us to the local science fiction convention that we are dressed for?"

"Snazzy alien-turtle outfits, huh?" Mikey said in his own version of a super-nerdy voice.

"Yep," Donnie chimed in. "We're just typical, normal humans who got lost in the middle of our normal, everyday human lives. Nailed it."

"Dude," Leo whispered to Donnie nervously, "you gotta make it to rehearsal."

"Give to me creature," demanded one of the joggers. He had a strange accent. "We are his owners."

But the little animal hissed and growled at them. No WAY were we handing him over.

"How you say 'pretty please or we'll destroy you'?" the other jogger asked.

Destroy us?!

Now I KNEW I wasn't giving these guys the weird little creature. "Forget it," I said. "If you know what's good for you, you'll leave. Nicely and quietly."

"You do not intimidate us," the first jogger snarled. He turned toward Donnie. "With or without your fake nerd voices."

"That was my real voice," Donnie protested.

"You better GET intimidated," Raph

warned. "'Cause we're like nothing you've ever seen!"

The jogger made an elaborate gesture. A weird glow passed over the two guys, and they transformed into these big warriors riding huge, snarling dogs! They were carrying, like, scepters! Whoa!

"Weapons ahoy!" Raph ordered, taking charge. He drew out his *sai* blades, which looked kind of like giant forks but with really sharp points and edges.

"We agreed to reserve 'ahoy' for ship-based adventures," Donnie reminded him. "I got this!"

He pressed a button on his *tech-bo* staff. It sprouted two rocket engines and started twirling ... out of control! It flew up into the air! "No!" Donnie cried.

POOF! The little animal disappeared from my arms! *POOF!* He reappeared in midair, right by Donnie's *tech-bo,* and clamped onto it with his teeth. *POOF!* He reappeared above Donnie and dropped the *tech-bo* right into his hands. "Hey," Donnie said, "he plays fetch!" *POOF!* The dog-thingy popped back into my arms. "And teleports!" he added. "OH MY GOSH—HE TELEPORTS?!"

The Turtles gave the two big warriors their best shots, even going into ninja mode, but the warriors kept blasting them with these weird waves of energy. They even destroyed three of the guys' weapons!

One of the warriors slammed his scepter onto the ground. A wave of energy knocked us all off our feet!

The other warrior threw a glowing ball of energy around the little animal so he couldn't teleport away.

"I have the agent and the vial!" he crowed.

The first warrior pulled out this glowing blue compass and traced a symbol in front of a brick wall. The bricks shifted and made this weird, scary-looking face with a wide-open mouth. The mouth was an opening into what looked like a mystical world!

CHAPTER TWO

"**W**HOOAA!" we all said at the same time, amazed.

Suddenly, a delivery guy rode around the corner on his bike. He swerved to avoid hitting us and went right into the opening! "WHOOAA!" he screamed.

I watched as one warrior rode his big dog into the opening. The other one dragged the little animal in! "The dog-cat thingy!" I cried, diving into the hole. "Let's go!"

But before the Turtles could follow me, the opening closed! (This is the part they told me about later.) It looked just like a regular brick wall again.

"April!" Raph yelled.

"I think she's okay," Leo said, "'cause there's no April bits on the ground."

"How do we get her out of there?" Raph asked.

"And equally important," Donnie asked, "WHERE is there?"

The symbol the warrior had drawn in the air was fading. Mikey quickly copied it onto his hand. "Hey, I've seen this before! In fact, we ALL have!"

Back in their lair, the Turtles stared at a compass in a case next to the TV. It had the symbol on it! "Let's ask Splinter for that compass," Raph said. "It's the key!"

Mikey shook his head. "We can't disturb the master in the middle of his favorite Japanese game show."

Their father, Splinter, a mysterious old rat, was lying on a couch watching a show called *Soapy Treadmill.* He had on a snack hat that funneled chips into his mouth.

"Hey, Pop," Leo said to him. "Any chance me and the guys here could have the living room tonight?"

Laughing hysterically, Splinter wheezed, "And I thought Purple was the funny one!"

"I TOLD you guys I was the funniest," Donnie said seriously.

Using his feet, Splinter took a can of cheese out of a mini fridge and sprayed cheese on a cracker already in his mouth.

"What if I moved the TV so you could

watch in bed?" Donnie suggested.

"No, my butt is asleep, just how I like it," Splinter rasped.

The Turtles huddled behind the couch. Raph laid out an elaborate plan for getting the compass. "Mikey, you distract Splinter by faking an accident. Donnie, you cut down on visibility by blowing smoke out of your lab. I'll rappel in from the ceiling.

"What's Leo doing?" Mikey asked.

"Getting the compass," Leo said, holding it up.

"What?! How'd you get that?" Raph asked, astonished.

Leo shrugged. "You know he always passes out after milk and cake."

His brothers looked at Splinter. Sure enough, he was snoring heavily, with a milk mustache and frosting on his face.

"Let's go find April," Leo said.

CHAPTER THREE

Back at the construction site, Raph nervously held the compass, ready to draw the symbol in the air with it.

"You can do it, Raph!" Mikey said. "Remember, if you don't, we'll lose our best friend forever!"

"Don't say that!" Leo warned his brother. "You know Raph chokes under pressure!"

Raph started to sweat.

"Leo!" Donnie snapped. "Raph's even

more self-conscious when you talk about it! And then you can smell his fear!"

"Stop talking about my fear stink!" Raph ordered. "I'm already so sweaty I can barely hold this thing!"

Raph tried drawing the symbol in front of the wall, but nothing happened. He tried again. And again. And quickly twice more. Nothing! He punched the wall. *WHAM!*

"Stupid wall!" Raph muttered.

"How 'bout we let the artist of the crew take a poke at it?" Mikey asked, reaching for the compass.

Raph handed it to him. Mikey closed his eyes, took a deep breath, and drew the design.

The wall opened!

"It worked!" Donnie cried.

"All I had to do was believe in myself," Raph said, leaping into the mystic hole.

His brothers looked at each other, then followed. *WHOOSH!* They were pulled in!

"OOF!" The four brothers landed in a pile on a rooftop with a view of the city.

But not New York.

It was the Hidden City, a mysterious place deep below the city we all knew and loved. Giant crystals and glowing fungi lit up the bizarre place.

The Turtles got to their feet and stared in disbelief. Mikey sniffed. "I can smell Raph's amazement stink."

I stepped out of my hiding place. "Hey, guys! Over here!"

"April!" Mikey cried. "You're okay!"

We all hugged.

"Where are we?" Raph asked.

"I've been exploring," I said. "It's a mystic hidden city deep under New York!"

"Omigosh!" Mikey cried.

Leo covered Mikey's mouth. "So where's the dog-cat thingy?"

CHAPTER FOUR

I led the Turtles down into the building. From an atrium, we could spy on the lab where the little animal was caged in tangled branches held together by a mystic field.

The delivery guy was caged there, too. "If you're the guy who keeps calling about the calamari," he called out, "fine, it's pig butts. But the crab cakes are real!"

A wall of vines opened and a big weird-looking dude with sheep horns came in.

Gargoyles jumped off his shoulders and ran to the cages. "I assure you, I have no interest in your petty cakes of crab," the dude sneered.

He patted a bizarre contraption with a swarm of bugs flying inside it. "You should be proud," he told the delivery guy. "You are about to be part of an experiment that will change the very nature of humanity!"

"I just want a reasonable tip," the guy said. "And to get out of this cage."

Sheep-horned guy took the vial off the little animal's collar and poured some pink liquid into the machine. So THAT was why the warriors snatched the dog-cat thingy! For his vial full of weird pink liquid! The liquid flowed through tubes and turned into glowing green ooze!

"This dude looks like serious trouble," I whispered to the Turtles.

"Yeah," Raph agreed. "And if I've learned anything from *Jupiter Jim* shows, glowing green usually equals bad."

The bugs sucked up the green ooze. Their stomachs glowed. The big guy with the sheep horns plucked a bug out of the air and carried it over to the delivery guy.

"Is this gonna hurt?" the delivery guy asked nervously.

"It will," the bad dude answered. "If I'm doing it right."

He put the bug right on the delivery guy's face. The bug shot the delivery guy with glowing green goo . . . and he mutated! His arms, legs, and body stretched, getting longer, until he was a big fishy mutant made from pink-and-white sticks of imitation crab! He yelled and ran out of the lab.

"Should we go after him, boss?" asked one of the gargoyles.

But their boss just smiled. "The mutation worked. Exactly like it did all those years ago."

Up in the atrium, Raph whispered, "Mutation? Like us? Could we be—"

"Part imitation crab?" Mikey asked.

"No, Mikey," Donnie said. "But it would explain the rather astounding coincidence that Splinter had the key to opening a gateway that led directly to this recently reopened mutation lab."

The little animal growled at the weirdo.

"I'll deal with you next," he threatened.

I turned to the Turtles. "We can't let that sheep-horned weirdo do anything to that dog!"

"Except for Donnie, we're out of weapons," Leo pointed out.

Donnie smirked. "Next time, make your weapons out of high-grade titanium."

Raph jumped to his feet and lectured his brothers. "Guys! Who needs weapons? We're ninjas! Leo's got his mad skills. No one flips better than Mikey. Donnie's got that big old brain. And I've got—"

I bumped Raph aside and finished his sentence for him. "—a friend who knows where there's a room full of weapons!"

I took them to the weapons chamber I'd found earlier. The guys were thrilled! They were reaching for weapons when Raph said, "Yo, guys! How 'bout we take the glowy ones?"

He pointed toward a case of luminescent weapons. The Turtles' eyes bugged out.

"Dibs on the sword!" Leo called, grabbing the shining *odachi* blade.

"Cowabunga!" Mikey cried as he grabbed a glimmering spiked ball on a chain called a *kusari-fundo.*

"Boom!" Raph shouted, knocking two glowing *tonfa* sticks together. "Hoo-ah!"

I noticed Donnie studying his *tech-bo* staff. "What about you, Donnie? Don't you want a glowy weapon?"

"No, I'm good," he said. I heard him whisper "I'll never let you go" to his beloved *tech-bo*. Then he noticed a purple lens hovering over a stand. "This looks interesting, though," he said, taking the gemlike lens.

"All right!" Raph grinned. "Now let's go save that dog-cat thingy!"

CHAPTER FIVE

The mean little gargoyles poked at the dog-cat thingy with sticks, snickering. It growled at them but couldn't teleport out of its jail. Nearby, the creepy horned guy examined a glowing bug under a large lens. "Perfect. Still has plenty of ooze left."

We burst in, waving our new weapons.

"All right," Raph announced, "you unusually buff bookworm—"

"You're beautiful!" the dude gasped when

he saw the Turtles.

"Uh, thanks?" Raph said. "Give us the little guy, and you'll walk out of here with your horns still attached!"

"Shouldn't we also stop him from making crab men?" Leo pointed out.

"Okay," Raph agreed. "Give us the little guy, stop making crab men—"

"Imitation-crab men," Donnie corrected him.

"Okay, good note," Raph said. "Stop creating imitation-crab men—"

"And give us a ride home! In a limo! With a hot tub! And pizza!" Mikey added.

"Let's do this!" I interrupted, tired of speeches. I jumped in with my weapon held high. "APRIL O'NEIL!"

"Omigosh!" Mikey cried. "She just ran in!"

I charged the cage. The gargoyles swooped at me, but I swung my shillelagh (this big knobby stick I'd found in the weapons chamber) at them. The Turtles went for the horned weirdo, but he threw these strange pods into the air. Giant vines grew and tripped up the Turtles! It was as if the horned guy was controlling the vines! Then he threw rocks onto the floor that grew into a giant rock golem monster! It roared as it attacked the Turtles.

Using their new weapons, the Turtles managed to destroy the rock golem monster. I thought the horned weirdo would be mad, but instead he said, "Impressive! Clearly, mutants can be as tough as I'd hoped!"

"Oh, well, great," Leo said. "And since you're surrendering—"

"Baron Draxum does not surrender," the weirdo growled.

"Well, when he gets here, we'll deal with

him," Leo said. But then he realized the scary guy was talking about himself and laughed. "Ohhh, I see. You're doing that sinister talking-in-the-third-person thing."

"Only Raph can use the third person!" Raph growled. "All right, guys, time to put our training to use!"

"What training?" Leo asked, puzzled. "You guys have been training?"

As I dealt with the two gargoyles, the Turtles battled Baron Draxum. Just as the four of them were about to simultaneously whack him with their new weapons, he slammed the ground, sending out a shock wave that knocked them off their feet!

"Ha!" he cried triumphantly. "And that's why Baron Draxum—"

BONK! One of the gargoyles landed right on his head. "Sorry, boss," it apologized.

I was still fighting the gargoyles with my

shillelagh when Baron Draxum blasted me across the room with a ball of energy!

"You did NOT just do that to our friend!" Mikey shouted. He spun his new weapon . . . and it started to glow! He tried to whip it at Baron Draxum, but it stretched all the way across the huge chamber! "Magic weapon!" Mikey called, amazed, as the *kusari-fundo* yanked him behind it, sending him bouncing around the hall like a ball in a pinball machine! *WHACK!* Mikey crashed into the baron's big machine full of green bugs!

CHAPTER SIX

"Whoa! Mikey, that was awesome!" Raph said, amazed. "How'd you do that?"

Mikey shrugged. "I don't know, man. I was just swinging my weapon like this, and all of a sudden–"

As Mikey swung his *kusari-fundo*, it glowed with mystic power.

Suddenly, the weapon zoomed off, dragging him with it again.

"Let me try!" Raph said, spinning his

tonfa sticks and chanting "Magic weapon!" over and over. Power surged through his weapon, knocking him back into a wall!

Leo spun his sword and charged at the baron. But the sword's mystic power suddenly opened up two strange portals—one below Leo and one above—and he kept falling in the bottom hole and reappearing out of the top hole! "Get me off this ride!" he yelled.

Donnie switched his *tech-bo* to mallet mode. "And that's why I like fighting the old-fashioned way—with impossibly futuristic high-tech weaponry!"

He managed to hit Baron Draxum a few times. But then Mikey, still flying around the room, slammed into Donnie and knocked him into Raph. Leo continued to loop through the two magic portals.

Baron Draxum stared at the floundering

Turtles, shaking his head. "You fight like untrained buffoons, but under me you could become true warriors." He threw small pods at us that expanded, trapping us all in cocoons!

"How are we gonna save the dog-cat thingy now?" I asked.

"Donnie's on it," Donnie said, lowering his goggles and scanning the room. A readout in his high-tech goggles told him that Draxum's mutation machine, cracked from Mikey's collision, was about to explode!

"Turtles," the baron said, "why are you trying to stop my plans? We are all in this together."

"I don't know if this is part of your plan," Donnie said, "but your lab's about to explode."

Energy surged through the mutation machine and . . . *BOOM!*

"Aw, nuts," Baron Draxum muttered as a huge chunk of the machine fell on him. The glowing mutation bugs were released, flying everywhere!

Another piece of debris fell on the dog-cat thingy's cage, freeing him. *POOF!* He appeared right next to me! "Little guy," I asked urgently, "can you do your thing and get us out of here?"

The creature gave a little meow and . . . *POOF!* We were out of the lab! Mikey whipped out Splinter's compass and drew the symbol on the wall, and the mystic portal opened! We jumped through!

Back at the construction site, we fell out of the portal—into New York, safe and sound. Splinter's compass fell to the ground and broke. "Oh no!" Mikey cried. "Splinter's doohickey!"

The dog-cat thingy dropped right into my arms. "Are you okay, boy? Or girl? You sure were good through all that mayhem. Hey! Mayhem. That's a cute name!"

Raph struck a pose. "We just defeated a boss villain! We're heroes! We deserve a name . . . like . . . Mad Dogs!"

"Mad Dogs?" Leo asked. "You don't think something like Ninja Mutant Turtle Teens—er, I don't know. We'll keep brainstorming."

Just then, a swarm of the mutation bugs with the glowing green stomachs came out of the portal and flew off in different directions.

"Huh," Donnie said, watching them go. "That can't be good."

Donnie's Gifts

CHAPTER ONE

Hey, if April can tell a story, so can I. It's me, Leo, here to tell you about the time Donnie gave me, Raph, and Mikey some presents.

It wasn't Christmas or our birthdays, or even Give Your Brothers Some Rad Presents Day. Donnie just thought the three of us could use some improvement—well, I'm getting ahead of myself. Here's what happened. . . .

The whole thing started in an alley here in New York City. I don't know if you've ever been in a New York alley, but it ain't pretty. Garbage, cockroaches, rats ... and those are the NICE parts!

On this particular night, we were battling some mutant bugs with long stingers like the kind you see on scorpions. And if you're seeing scorpions regularly, remind me not to visit your house. I guess these bugs are called silverfish, which is really weird, 'cause they're not fish; they're bugs. I'm not kidding. Look it up on your phone.

But, like I said, these weren't regular silverfish bugs—they were MUTANT silverfish, about the size of a human!

I was pretty busy fighting, but I looked over and saw Raph bashing one of the bugs . . . and it split into two smaller silverfish! He bashed another one! *WHAM!* That one split into two smaller ones, too!

Donnie yelled at Raph. "Every time you smash them, they just split into two!"

"I know," Raph said, grinning. "Isn't it cool?" He smashed another one. Two bugs.

"Think, Raph," Donnie urged.

Raph thought for a second. Then his eyes widened. "Ohhh," he said, realizing. "I guess it DOES double the problem." He grinned again. "Which means double the smashing!"

Donnie rolled his eyes. Raph kept smashing the silverfish until they were swarming all over, stinging him like crazy.

"Check your fists at the door, Raph," Mikey called. "This situation calls for a dose of my psycho-acrobatics!"

"No, no, no!" Donnie warned.

But Mikey wasn't listening. He was too

excited about jumping and flipping into action. He did a handspring, bounced off a wall, and used his *kusari-fundo* to catch some bugs and fling them into a garbage container. Then he tried to cartwheel through the air to close the lid, but his foot got caught on a fire escape, and he ended up falling into the container with the silverfish! The lid slammed closed!

"GYAAAH!" Mikey screamed. "They're in my shell! The pain! The *paaain*!"

"I got you, buddy!" I called to him. I opened the container, yanked Mikey out, and shook the bugs out of his shell. With my *odachi*, I sliced open a fire hydrant. The water blasted the bugs away!

This called for one of my brilliant one-liners.

"Looks like those bugs are all washed up!" I said.

"BOOOO!" Mikey jeered.

"Okay," I said. "How about this? Those bugs are so wet—"

"Leo!" Donnie yelled.

"No, no, this is a good one," I promised. "You ask, 'How wet are they?' And I go—"

WHAM!

Apparently, The silverfish came back, slamming into us, stingers first! They WEREN'T all washed up! Mikey, Raph, and I were struggling with the silverfish that were swarming all over us. When we'd smashed them, they'd divided and gotten smaller, but they could still sting!

"Ugh, this is getting old," Donnie said, whipping out his *tech-bo* staff. He punched a button and blasted the bugs with goo. They ran off!

"They're getting away!" Mikey cried.

"Nice hustle, Donnie," Raph said. "I knew

we could deal with this as a team!"

"It was pretty much just me," Donnie pointed out. "But segue ... I think I've got a little something that'll kick our skills into high gear!"

CHAPTER TWO

We were all wondering what Donnie's "little something" could be. He tapped on this watch-doohickey he wears called a wrist com. *ZZZZRT-SMASH!* A giant drill bit burst up through the street!

We all gasped, amazed! Mikey ran over to the drill and hugged it, saying, "It's beautiful!"

"No," Donnie said impatiently. "Not the drill bit . . ."

I was amazed. "That's not the thing you wanted to show us? That should TOTALLY be the thing!"

"I'm still working on the drill bit," Donnie said. "It's just the delivery system. The real thing is much more personal and thoughtful." He looked excited and nervous. "I hope you like it. If you don't, I'll be crushed."

Raph put his arm around Donnie. "Just show us what it is. I'm sure we'll love it!"

"All right," Donnie said. "Here goes."

I couldn't believe we were just moving past the giant drill like it was nothing.

Donnie pressed more buttons on his forearm thingamabob. *BRZZZZ.* The drill bit opened. Inside was a red helmet with a monitor, an orange jumpsuit, and a blue electronic collar with flashing lights!

"Whoa, I'm jazzed!" Raph said, picking up the helmet.

"You even got my life colors right!" Mikey said, pulling on the jumpsuit.

"I don't know what this is," I said as I grabbed the collar, "but it's got a lot of blinkity-blinks."

"I'm so glad you like them!" Donnie said. "Now let me show you how they work. . . ."

But as Raph and I put on the helmet and the collar, we heard a loud shriek from the alley. "What was that?" Raph said.

We ran into the alley and saw a huge, hulking mutant pig dressed like a chef! He had ears like a pig; cruel, beady eyes; a turned-up snout; and a gaping mouth full of sharp teeth. He was whacking a silverfish with a meat mallet!

"That guy looks like the meat sweats!" Raph said. "Like when you eat a lot of meat and start sweating!"

Raph was right. We all laughed.

Meat Sweats tossed the mutant silverfish into a bag, lifted a grate, and jumped into a tunnel. We followed him to this weird underground "kitchen," an old subway car he'd outfitted with cooking equipment, and hid behind some barrels to see what he was doing. He was sprinkling ingredients on the mutant silverfish and talking to himself about how he'd cook it. "Mmm, a little salt. Pinch of savory. Lemon for the tang. Unleash the flavor!"

"'Unleash the flavor'?" Mikey snapped his fingers. "Omigosh, it's Rupert Swaggart!"

"Oh yeah!" Raph said, nodding. Then he looked confused. "Who's that?"

CHAPTER THREE

"The celebrity chef!" Mikey explained.

We still had no idea who he was talking about.

"On TV? The host of *Chef's Nightmare*? You know, that show where he screams at chefs until they give up their dreams? I love that guy!"

Mikey told us that a few weeks ago, he'd seen an episode of *Chef's Nightmare* where a bug had flown into the studio and stung Rupert—one of those weird green glowing bugs from Baron Draxum's lab. "He sprouted pigs' ears and a snout! The audience freaked! It was pretty much their best episode ever!"

"You saw a celebrity chef transform into a mutant pig and you didn't tell anyone?" Donnie asked. He couldn't believe it.

"I didn't want to burn my risotto!" Mikey said.

We watched, horrified, as Meat Sweats reached toward the pot of simmering mutant silverfish.

"He's not going to EAT that bug, is he?" Donnie whispered. But Meat Sweats didn't eat the bug. He pulled off one of his gloves, revealing tentacles instead of fingers! He wrapped his tentacles around the silverfish, and a weird green essence flowed up into his arm! He was absorbing the silverfish's powers! His eyes glowed green! Gross.

"That's SO MUCH WORSE!" Donnie said.

Meat Sweats inhaled deeply. "Ah, I feel the rush of your delicious energy!" Then he sniffed again, harder. "Am I picking up the delightful aroma of mutant with an after-stench of turtle?"

He looked in our direction. "I'm thinking Lime Turtle Tenderloin over a bed of saffron rice. Brilliant!"

"Ooh, that sounds good!" Mikey said.

"He's talking about eating us!" Donnie exclaimed.

"Excuse me for wanting to be eaten in style!" Mikey said.

Raph waved his hand in front of their faces. "Hey, you two! Focus! It's time to mash this pig's potatoes!" He ran right at Meat Sweats with his fist cocked.

But he heard a voice come from his new

helmet. "Your opponent is quite strong. Perhaps you should reevaluate."

"What the . . . ?" Raph asked. "This helmet talks?"

The helmet's visor showed a meter comparing Raph's brain use to his muscle power. Distracted by the display, Raph got walloped by Meat Sweats's mallet. *WHAM!* He tumbled back to us and staggered to his feet.

"Donnie," he said, "this helmet's talking to me!"

"Great!" Donnie said. "It's working!"

Raph shook off his dizziness and charged right back at Meat Sweats.

"Charging the enemy?" the helmet said in its calm voice. "Consider other options."

"You again?" Raph said. "How's this for options? SMASH AND BASH!"

He punched Meat Sweats, landing a

powerful blow. But the mutant pig divided into tiny versions of himself, each with its own tiny meat mallet! He'd taken on the silverfish's ability to multiply with every punch!

That was all we needed—MORE Meat Sweats!

CHAPTER FOUR

The mini Meat Sweats ran straight at Raph, waving their tiny mallets. "Time to unleash the flavor!" they yelled in their little squeaky voices. They pounded Raph all over with their meat mallets.

"Ow!" Raph cried. "Stop it! Ouch!"

We watched the little jerks, amazed.

"Fascinating," Donnie said. "Meat Sweats must have absorbed the silverfish's powers! He can divide and replicate!"

The army of mini pigs charged right toward us. Mikey yelled, "Flee!" And we took off down the subway tunnel as fast as we could. But the mini pigs grabbed Donnie and dragged him off!

When the mini pigs were getting close to Mikey, he started to go into one of his acrobatic routines, jumping and flipping. But as he was about to kick off the wall of a tunnel, an alarm went off! *WEET! WEET! WEET!*

"Danger," warned a computer voice from his new orange jumpsuit. "Impact warning."

"Huh?" Mikey asked, confused.

The jumpsuit inflated! It was like he was stuck inside a big bouncy ball! When Mikey hit the floor, he bounced back up in the air. "What the . . . ?" Mikey said. "This suit totally messed up my steez!"

("Steez," by the way, is "style" plus

"ease." Just in case you didn't know. You're welcome.)

I was battling my own troop of mini pigs, but I was doing all right. One of the mini pigs climbed up on me and pounded my neck and shoulders with his little mallet. I flicked him off, sending him into the air.

"You'll beat me . . . ," I said, whacking another mini pig with the back of my sword, hitting it like a golf ball. It sailed through the air and smacked into the other mini pig. ". . . when pigs fly!"

ZZZZAP!

"Ow!" I yelled, feeling the sting of an electric shock. "What the cheese was that?"

I realized I'd been shocked by the collar Donnie had made for me. *Must have a malfunction,* I thought. I raised my fist to pound the mini pigs. "These little piggies are gonna cry wee-wee-wee–"

ZZZZAP!

Shocked again! "OW!" I shouted. "This thing doesn't like my one-liners?"

WHOMP! Mikey fell right on top of me in his inflated suit! I got out from underneath him, and we managed to put a subway train between us and the mini pigs.

"Dude! Mikey, what'd you do?" I asked.

"I dunno!" he said. "It's this suit! Every time I do some razzmatazz, this thing inflates and throws me off my game! I need my razz AND my tazz!"

I explained how my collar zapped me every time I made a joke. Popping up behind us, Raph complained that his helmet kept nagging him.

"Does Donnie really think I'm a crazy kangaroo who needs to wear a padded suit so I don't hurt myself?" Mikey asked.

"Does he really think I need to be told what to do all the time?" Raph asked.

"And who doesn't love my one-liners?" I asked. "They fire up the team! Right, guys?" For some reason, Mikey and Raph just looked down and kicked the ground.

I figured they didn't hear me. Too many roaring subways. And squealing mini pigs.

CHAPTER FIVE

"Well, anyway," I said, "we need to tell Donnie that he doesn't get to tell us what to be."

"Yeah, I know," Raph agreed. "But he's such a softshell. . . ."

"It's like he's trying to fix us!" I insisted. "Are we broken?"

"No!" Raph and Mikey shouted together.

Mikey turned to Raph. "So what are you gonna do about it, leader? You gonna stand up and tell him his gifts stink?"

Raph got a determined look on his face. "Yeah! I think I AM!"

His phone rang. He whipped it out and saw Donnie's face on the screen. "It's him."

Mikey grinned. "Oh, he's SOOOOO gonna get it!"

But Raph suddenly changed his tone and cooed into the phone, "Hey, buddy! Really loving the gifts you got us!"

Mikey and I couldn't believe Raph had chickened out! He was supposed to give it to Donnie straight! And here he was telling him we LOVED his gifts!

"What's that?" Raph said. "Hang on—I'm gonna put you on speaker." He pressed a button, and Donnie's voice rang out: "AIIIGGGHH! WHERE'D YOU GUYS GO?! THEY'RE ALL OVER ME! THEY'RE GONNA COOK ME ALIVE!"

The phone went dead.

"You need to save him," Raph's helmet said.

"NO DUH!" Raph bellowed. We raced off to save our brother.

Back in Meat Sweats's kitchen, the mini pigs had knocked Donnie out and tied him to a rod. They put the rod on a rotisserie over glowing charcoal! Then the mini pigs reformed themselves into full-sized Meat Sweats, who seasoned Donnie. "Mmm, a delicate softshell!"

Raph whispered to us, "Okay, according to Donnie's gift, I'm supposed to make a plan."

"Okay," I said. "Whaddya got?"

We all just stood there a moment.

"I'm not good at making plans!" Raph blurted out.

"Of course you're not!" Mikey agreed. "And I'm not good at fighting if I can't razzmatazz!"

"And I'm not good at suppressing my lightning wit," I added.

"The point is," Raph said, "we gotta be US! LIKE THIS!"

We dashed into the room where Meat Sweats was chopping vegetables for his roast. Mikey used a little distraction-jitsu.

"Hey, Meat Sweats!" he yelled, and threw some shadow puppets on the wall. Meat Sweats looked up, confused.

Raph grabbed Donnie off the spit, threw him over his shoulder, and ran for it.

"C'mon back!" Meat Sweats shouted. "I used an entire pound of butter on him!"

Then I yanked off my collar and threw

it down the big pig's pants. "Hey, Meat Sweats! Looks like you're about to get some shocking news!"

ZZZZAP!

"I love the smell of frying bacon in the morning!"

ZZZZAP!

Meat Sweats was shocked by the collar. "I must admit," he said, dazed, "I do smell delicious. . . ."

CHAPTER SIX

Donnie started to come to. "What are you doing?"

"Getting the most out of your gift!" I explained. "Meat Sweats is getting a little hot under his—"

POW! The mutant pig nailed me with his mallet!

"I get it, Leo!" Mikey said. "These gifts can help, if we use them OUR WAY!"

He jumped up between two pipes,

right over Meat Sweats. His suit inflated, wedging him there. Then it deflated. As he fell, it inflated again! Mikey bounced Meat Sweats right into a pile of pots and pans, and then bounced safely away! "RAZZ, MAZZ, and TAZZ!" Mikey cheered.

But Meat Sweats wasn't done. He crawled out and came at me with his mallet. I gave him another jolt with the collar. "Hey, Meat Sweats! I hear baloney is full of YOU!"

ZZZZAP!

While the mutant pig recovered from the shock, Raph raced toward him.

"Wait, Raphael," his helmet warned. "You need a plan."

"Gah!" Raph groaned. He pulled the helmet off his head, put it on his fist, and charged Meat Sweats.

"Bad plan!" warned the helmet.

WHAM!

Raph slammed into Meat Sweats with everything he had! "Cowabunga!" he cried.

The pig rocketed down a tunnel. We heard a subway train blast its horn, and then the train came zooming out of the tunnel with Meat Sweats plastered across its front.

"Ah, rubbish!" he yelled as he rode off into the distance.

We ran to Donnie and cut him off the rotisserie spit.

"Donnie," Raph said, grinning, "your gifts really brought out the best in us!"

"I'm funnier!" I agreed, nodding.

"I'm bouncier!" Mikey added.

"And I'm smashier!" Raph concluded. "Your gifts are the stuff!"

"But you were supposed to . . . ," Donnie started. Then he stopped. "Ah, forget it. You guys are great the way you are. Bring it in! Group hug!"

Victorious and proud, we pulled each other together into a hug. But then heard Mikey's suit warn, "Impact imminent!"

POP!

His suit inflated, and we all went flying!

REPO
MANTIS

CHAPTER ONE

And now, get ready for a story from me, MIKEY! It's about how Donnie and I ended up working for a mutant mantis. But I'm getting ahead of myself. Let's start at the very beginning. . . .

You know how Donnie loves to put together all these super incredible gadgets and whatchamacallits? Well, he's gotta get the parts somewhere. And more often than not, that somewhere is this smelly dump out in Queens. Queens is a section of New York City. Sounds fancy, but it's not—at least, not the place we were in.

"Man, junkyards are gold mines!" Donnie cried enthusiastically as he dug into a wrecked car. He was wearing one of his battle shells—the one he'd outfitted with telescoping robot arms. He used one of the arms to hold up an air freshener shaped like a pineapple. "Who needs real pineapples when you have one of these babies?"

I noticed something overhead. "Donnie, I really think we should—"

He pulled out a pair of big fuzzy dice. Each dice had twelve sides, the kind you'd use in a role-playing game, if you liked that sort of thing. Which Donnie does.

"Fuzzy nerd dice!" Donnie shouted. "Score!"

"DONNIE!" I yelled, yanking him out of the car so he could see what I'd seen.

Above us, a huge magnet released a crushed car. As it fell right toward us, we jumped out of the way. *WHAM!* It fell on top of a big stack of smashed cars.

"OOF!" We landed on the ground next to the car pile.

"Mikey, next time, I'd appreciate a heads-up," Donnie said.

"Okay," I said. "Heads-up."

"You're a little late," Donnie complained.

"No, I mean over there," I explained, pointing.

A tow truck drove into the junkyard. On its side it said REPO MANTIS SALVAGE. It was belching smoke out of its exhaust pipes. We took cover so the driver wouldn't see us.

Then we saw what the truck was towing.

"Is that . . . ?" I asked, amazed.

"It is!" Donnie said, thrilled.

It was the moon buggy from our favorite sci-fi series, *Jupiter Jim*!

"Featured in not one, not two, but SIXTY sequels to *Jupiter Jim's Last Trip to the Moon*!" Donnie squealed.

VROOM! The tow truck peeled out, hit a one-eighty, and flung the moon buggy, parking it perfectly right next to a row of junked cars and trucks.

"How could anybody let that historical gem slip through their fingers?" I wondered.

"I don't know," Donnie said, "but we gotta have it!"

We stealthily made our way closer to the buggy, crouching behind a car. "How are we gonna get the buggy?" I asked. "We can't go up and talk to one of those human people."

CREEEAAAK! The car we were hiding behind rose up in the air. We saw this giant praying mantis mutant lifting the car with its forelegs! He had long, sharp claws on his feet, bulging eyes, and antennae sticking out of his head.

"Who the heck are you?" he asked us.

"GAAAAH!" I screamed.

"MUTANT!" Donnie yelled.

CHAPTER TWO

"Wait," Donnie said. "We're mutants, too. I take back that scream."

"Dude, you'd better hide!" I warned the mutant bug. "There's a human guy around here with a tow truck!"

"Easy, easy," he said, patting the air with his forelegs. "Calm down. That's MY truck. I'm Repo Mantis. The guy is me."

"This is YOUR junkyard?" I asked. "You HAVE to sell us that moon buggy."

Donnie pulled me aside and whispered, "Whoa, cool your scramjets. It's a negotiation. To get the best price, we gotta play this *smooooooth*." Looking like he didn't care about the moon buggy at all, Donnie slipped on sunglasses, strolled over and dragged his finger through the dust on its hood. "So, how much'll you pay us to take this pile of parts off your hands?"

Repo Mantis ignored him and checked his clipboard. "Hmm, running low on fenders . . ."

"I see you drive a hard bargain," Donnie said. "Perhaps I can interest you in a little coin?" He pulled out his coin purse and dug inside. "I've got big silver and small silver, and I can make it rain copper!" He tossed a few pennies in the air, then quickly bent over and picked them back up.

Repo Mantis rolled his eyes. "You ain't

got nearly enough. But I could use a couple of tough muties like you. Ever do any repo work?"

"Of course!" I lied. "What's repo work?"

"It's when you take stuff back from deadbeats who didn't pay for it," Repo Mantis grumbled. "Do a job for me today, and I'll give ya that moon buggy."

"We're in!" I exclaimed.

Looking worried, Donnie took me aside. "Look, Mikey, repo men have to be mean. And I don't know if you know this, but you're kind of a softy."

"Hey, that really hurts my feelings!" I cried. Donnie gave me a look. "Oh, wait— you're right. But I can do this. Hard as nails!" I growled, and said to Repo Mantis in my best tough voice, "What's the skinny, *chico*?"

"Need ya to get a camper from a real

shady mutant," he explained. "Holes up in the woods on the WRONG side of the tracks, in the DARKEST outskirts of the BAD part of town."

"If you're trying to scare us, it's not, working," Donnie scoffed. "But please stop."

CHAPTER THREE

Soon we were walking through this really spooky forest. Wolves howled! Creepy shadows loomed! Twigs snapped! Because we stepped on them.

"I ran a profile on this guy," Donnie said. "Lawless loner, doesn't pay his bills, lives in these creepy woods—a ninety-eight percent match for that maniac I read about in the newspaper—the Spine-Breaking Bandit!"

I snorted. "I'm not scared of some

no-good forest-liver. Let's see him!" I spotted his camper. "There's his camper!"

The dude stuck his head out of the door and yawned. We saw gigantic teeth!

"YAAAH!" we screamed.

"That's the biggest forest-liver I've ever seen!" I gasped.

"He's totally gonna break our spines!" Donnie said. "Maybe we should call Raph and Leo."

"No!" I said. "We got this! Think of all the boss adventures we could have in the moon buggy."

"Okay," Donnie sighed. "If you're dead set on doing this, we gotta go stealth. Sneak-jitsu 101: never let a spine-breaker get behind you."

A flashlight snapped on.

"GAAAAH!" we screamed. "He's behind us!"

We ran, and a pack of wild dogs chased

us, barking like they wanted to eat us! We slammed to a stop when we crashed into the camper door—there was nowhere else to run! The door creaked open, and we looked up to see a gigantic shadowy figure. This was the end for us! But then the shadowy creature stepped into the light, and we were stunned to see the biggest, cutest, furriest mutant capybara ever. He was adorable. (By the way, Donnie explained to me what a capybara is. It's basically a super-cute rodent from South America.) And even cuter, he was cuddling a puppy!

"I'm Todd!" the mutant said in a gentle voice. "Welcome to Cuddlecakes Puppy Rescue, the puppiest place on earth!"

We came out of the bushes with our weapons ready. There were puppies everywhere.

"Puppies?" Donnie asked suspiciously.

"Which one are you having for lunch?"

"Oh, right!" Todd said. "It's lunchtime!" He pulled a rope, and dog food spilled into a trough. Puppies ran up and started eating, their little tails wagging happily.

"Aww!" I said. It was cuteness overload!

"You guys want some of my famous lemonade?" Todd offered. "I donate it to folks in Alaska who need a little sunshine." He poured us a couple of glasses.

It was delicious! Donnie took me aside and whispered, "Cute puppies? Lemonade? This is no Spine-Breaking Bandit!"

I agreed. "He's the nicest guy in the world."

"But we gotta be tough with him!" Donnie reminded me. "Hard as nails!"

"Got it," I said. I turned back to the mutant capybara. "So, Todd, let's get down to business about your camper."

"Sure thing!" Todd said. "Could you hold this little guy?"

He handed me an adorable puppy. It licked my face. "Aww, you little mischief maker!" I cooed. Then I got serious again. "Wait! We're supposed to be talking about your camper!"

"No prob!" Todd said agreeably. He pointed to the way I was holding the puppy. "You know, you're a natural!"

"I am?" I said, pleased. Then I remembered I was supposed to get tough. "Of course I am!" I growled.

For some reason, Donnie rolled his eyes.

CHAPTER FOUR

"**L**ook, Todd," Donnie said sternly. "You haven't made a payment in two years, and—"

"Yeah," Todd interrupted, nodding. "Turns out all you get for rescuing puppies are million-dollar smiles." He noticed a puppy on the ground next to Donnie who had rolled on her back. "Ooooh, looks like Miho wants her tummy rubbed!"

"What? No! I'm not here to rub Miho's tummy!" Donnie said. "I'm here to repo your camper with my hard-as-nails brother!"

He gestured toward me, but unfortunately at that moment I was bottle-feeding a bunch of the puppies. "And I'll call you Indiana Bones, and you—"

"Mikey, come on!" Donnie scolded.

"Oh, look!" Todd said to him. "Melvin wants to play! Would you mind giving his ball a little toss?"

Donnie looked down and saw a fluffy white puppy sitting up with a ball in its mouth. It wagged its tail, dropped the ball, and barked. *RUFF! RUFF!*

"Okay, fine," Donnie agreed. "I'll toss the ball if you give us the keys to your camper." He threw the ball, and the little puppy scrambled after it. But as Donnie threw the ball, he stepped forward. *SPLORT!*

"I'm in something squishy!" Donnie wailed. "I'm in something squishy!"

"Oh yeah," Todd said apologetically. "I'm so swamped with puppy and lemonade duties, I never get a chance to clean up the yard. But you guys are so good at this ... wanna grab a couple of shovels?"

Before we could say anything, Todd handed us two shovels.

Hours later, we finished dumping our last shovelfuls onto a truck. It drove off. Around us, the ground was spick-and-span. We leaned on our shovels, huffing and puffing.

"Why did we just do that?" I asked.

"I have no idea," Donnie said, wiping his brow. "It's like niceness is Todd's superpower."

Todd walked up, carrying a puppy in his arms. "The campground looks great, guys! You must be exhausted. Why don't you sleep over? In the morning, I can hold Sir Chomps-a-Lot while you floss his teeth!"

"No!" Donnie said firmly. "We didn't come here to help you. We came here to repossess your camper!"

"Oh, okay," Todd said in a supersad voice. He heaved a big sigh. "I guess me and the pups will just sleep under the stars tonight. And the next night. And the next . . ."

I felt tears springing into my eyes.

". . . and the next night, right into puppy hurricane season."

The wind blew. The puppy in Todd's arms whimpered.

I burst into tears. "I CAN'T DO IT!"

CHAPTER FIVE

Donnie sighed. I could tell he didn't want to put those puppies out in the cold any more than I did. "Okay, Todd. How about we build you and the puppies a nice place to sleep?"

Todd brightened up. "Really? And a place to feed the puppies? And to bathe them and diaper them and play with them?"

"Uh, sure," Donnie agreed, giving in to Todd's demands.

Todd hesitated. "I don't suppose you could—"

"Yes, there will be robot assistants!" Donnie snapped.

It wasn't easy, but Donnie and I built an absolutely killer place in the woods for Todd and his puppies to hang out. There was a maze for the puppies to run through. A machine that automatically flung disks to chase and catch. A self-cleaning fire hydrant. And of course, robots to feed and bathe the puppies.

Finally, we climbed into the camper, ready to claim our reward from Repo Mantis.

"Thanks, guys!" Todd called, waving. "I'll never forget you! And come back if you ever want to help—"

"NO!" Donnie shouted. He punched the gas and we peeled out of the campground, kicking up dust and rocks.

As we drove the repossessed camper into Repo Mantis's junkyard, Donnie and I sang the *Jupiter Jim* moon buggy song at the top of our lungs:

"We're taking a trip in the moon buggy.
One last trip to the moon, buddy.
It's the last trip in this vehicle,
At least until the next sequel!"

We screeched to a halt right in front of Repo Mantis and jumped out of the camper, psyched. "Hey, Repo!" I said. "One camper, as promised! Wax up that moon buggy!"

He looked past us at the camper, checking it out. "Not bad, not bad," he said in his tough-guy voice. "But what has happened is, I ain't giving the buggy to you."

"WHAT?!" I shouted.

"Turns out," Repo Mantis continued, "dorky *Jupiter Jim* fans'll pay big bucks just to sit in that thing. So I'm keepin' it." He turned and started to walk away.

"Hold it right there, pal!" Donnie said. "We had a deal!"

"Repo work is a tricky business, kids," Repo said, shrugging. "And you got tricked." He chuckled a weird, raspy chuckle.

We were supermad—all that work for nothing!

"We're not leaving here without our moon buggy!" Donnie insisted.

"Oh yeah?" Repo Mantis snarled. He jammed his forelegs into two blocks of smashed scrap metal. He held them up like boxing gloves. "I'm gonna break your legs halfway through, twice!"

He took a swing at Donnie, who blocked the punch with his *tech-bo* staff.

"Mikey, the crane!" Donnie shouted.

I knew just what he meant. I whipped my *kusari-fundo* at the crane's cab, hitting the switch to turn on the big magnet. Repo's metal cubes were yanked up to the magnet, taking him with it! *CLANK!* He hung in the air with his legs kicking.

We ran to the moon buggy and jumped in. Donnie floored it, and we pulled into the street. "Eat crater dust, Bug Man!" he yelled. Then he realized we weren't exactly flying down the road. "This thing is superslow!"

"Of course it is," I said. "It was built for the gravity of the moon."

Donnie shook his head. "That is wrong on so many levels."

CHAPTER SIX

*V*ROOOOM! Repo Mantis's tow truck came roaring after us, belching exhaust. *WHAM! WHAM! WHAM!* He slammed it right into us, rocking the moon buggy!

"GIVE ME BACK MY DORKMOBILE!" Repo bellowed.

I knew exactly what to do. "Moon core lasers, FIRE!" I punched the button on the buggy's control panel.

Nothing happened.

"Crater dust cloud! Zero-atmosphere Gatling missiles!" But every time I tried to fire one of the moon buggy's weapons, the plastic buttons just fell off the control panel. "Aww, nuts!"

"This is a movie vehicle," Donnie explained. "They wouldn't load it up with advanced lunar artillery."

I got an idea. "UNLESS ... it's the buggy from *Jupiter Jim's Third Last Trip to the Moon,* which had a fake dashboard to fool the Plutonians!"

I pulled off the dashboard. Underneath were gleaming switches! "Yeah! I'm kicking in Titan Turbo Mode!"

I hit the button and we blasted away! *ZOOM!*

But Repo Mantis was still driving his monstrous tow truck right at us! It was belching smoke as its chains swung wildly.

I hit the Gravity Grease 3000. Grease coated the road! The tow truck skidded but kept on coming. . . .

WHAM! Repo Mantis slammed into us again with his giant tow truck. I thought hard about which weapon might work best. . . .

"Hmm. Maybe the Bug Zapper?"

Donnie looked exasperated. "Why wouldn't you try that first?!"

"It didn't have a 3000 after it," I explained.

Donnie whipped out a marker and wrote "3000" next to the button. "Does it work for you now?"

"Oh yeah!" I said, hitting the button. A glowing blue orb launched out of the back of the moon buggy, right in Repo Mantis's path. He stared at the bright blue light, finding it irresistible.

"Oooooooh!" Repo Mantis said, loving the looks of that light.

He drove straight into it. *BVVVZZZZT!*

The Bug Zapper shocked Repo, and he lost control of his tow truck, driving into a brick wall. *SMASH!*

Donnie and I high-fived. "Hard as nails!" Donnie crowed as we peeled out in the moon buggy. *VROOOM!*

The Fast and the Furriest

CHAPTER ONE

This is Raph. Guess it's my turn to tell the next story. But first I gotta ask, if I'm the leader, SHOULDN'T I HAVE GONE FIRST?! WHY AM I TELLING THE LAST STORY?! Okay, now that I got that outta my system . . . story time! (And as usual, the parts I wasn't there for, I learned about later.)

It all started when Donnie dragged us into one of the sewer tunnels to show us his latest invention. He'd draped some shower curtains across the tunnel so we couldn't see what it was. He was really excited about it. And we were all curious—what had he made this time?

"You are about to witness my masterpiece!" he announced proudly. "My crowning glory! The greatest thing I've ever made! Gentlemen, behold the—"

"Is it the drill?" Leo guessed eagerly. "Is it that awesome drill you made when we were fighting the mutant silverfish?"

"Ah, no," Donnie said. "That's still in beta."

"LAME!" I yelled. With Donnie, it seems like everything is always "in beta." We wanted to see that drill again. We LOVED that drill!

"But this is better!" Donnie insisted. "MUCH better! I give you the—"

"Is it an even cooler, even bigger drill?" Mikey interrupted.

"NO! NO DRILL!" Donnie shouted. "THIS is the big surprise! Ta-stinkin'-da!"

He pulled down the curtain to reveal ... nothing!

Mikey was excited anyway. "Yay! A sewer tube full of nothing! I'm so proud of you!"

"What?!" Donnie yelled. "Where did it go?! I built us an amazing vehicle out of the *Jupiter Jim* moon buggy! Who stole our Turtle Tank?"

Though we didn't know it yet, at that very moment, our new Turtle Tank was screeching down a New York City street, knocking over a newspaper box. *WHAM!*

And guess who was driving it? (Spoiler

alert!) Our dear old dad, Splinter!

He was tearing up the town, his driver's window down, the wind blowing through his fur, howling, "HOT SOOOOUP!"

(That was our favorite action star, Lou Jitsu's, catchphrase.)

But we didn't know yet that Splinter had stolen it, so we took to the streets, trying to figure out what to do. "This is a real problem," I told Donnie. "Not only did they steal your tank thing—"

"Now you can finish the drill!" Mikey suggested.

"—but they also know where our lair is!" I pointed out. "It must be someone who's penetrated our inner circle!"

This stopped Donnie in his tracks. He thought of something. "Maybe even someone we've known for years!"

BAM! Donnie kicked in April's front door. We saw her putting curlers in Mayhem's fur. "WHERE'S OUR TURTLE TANK?!" Donnie demanded.

"Hi, Donnie!" April said sweetly. "You have nine seconds to tell me why you just broke my door."

Donnie pointed an accusing finger at her. "You're the only one who could have taken it!"

April whipped out a baseball bat and tapped it on her palm. "Three, two, one . . . "

CHAPTER TWO

*T*HUD! We hit the sidewalk outside April's apartment. She's tough, that girl. After all, she grew up in New York. And she hangs with us.

Donnie sat up, rubbing his jaw. "The good news is our inner circle is secure."

Mikey called up to one of April's windows. "Sorry, April! Movie night later?"

She leaned out. "Your treat," she said, and blew us a kiss.

"Who's our next suspect?" Donnie asked. Though we didn't notice at the time, Splinter was doing stunts in our Turtle Tank just a few blocks over, hooting and howling like a maniac.

I thought about who could possibly have stolen the Turtle Tank from our lair. "It's gotta be someone who knows we exist," I said.

"But who else do we know?" Mikey said. "Splinter!"

He pulled a wooden splinter out of his butt, not realizing that he'd accidentally nailed the culprit's name. "Must be from April's bat," Mikey said, tossing the splinter aside.

"It's gotta be another mutant," Leo said. "And I know where we can find a mutant— the mutant pizza place!"

He was talking about Run-of-the-Mill

Pizza, the restaurant where all the mutants hung out. We'd discovered it a few weeks before, amazed to learn that mutants have secret places in New York City that the humans know nothing about. The name's just a cover. The pizza's actually way above average.

"Good thinking!" Donnie said. "Let's go!"

We ran off, not realizing that Splinter was joyriding just a few yards away from us, the old rat!

When we reached Run-of-the-Mill Pizza, Leo had us huddle up before we went inside. "Okay, check this," he said. "We're gonna do the ol' 'Smooth Urban Cop Digging for Info in a Restaurant' routine."

Inside, Leo went straight up to a mutant

skeleton named Senor Hueso. "Say, Bone Man, you seem like you have your earhole to the ground. What do you know about a certain missing Turtle Tank?"

He stuffed something into the skeleton's hand. Hueso looked at it. "A coupon to Teddy Bear Town? No thanks." He crumpled it up.

Leo turned to a mutant who looked like a giant eyeball. "Hey, there, Green Eye," he said. "Know anything about a—"

SPLOOSH! She tossed her glass of water in his face. Dripping, he turned to a mutant baby and said, "Hey, wittle cutie, I bet you know—"

WHAP! The baby's scary eyes bugged out, and his giant tongue whacked Leo in the face!

Donnie couldn't take anymore. "ENOUGH WITH YOUR STUPID ROUTINE, LEO!" He confronted the mutants, trying to act tough. "I'm finding out which one of you wise guys took our tank, or I'm smashing everything in this dump!" He grabbed a table and tried to flip it over. But it was too heavy. Donnie grunted and strained as the mutants watched.

Senor Hueso pointed a finger bone at Donnie. "Your bad cop routine leaves something to be desired."

"Oh, we're not the police," Mikey said honestly.

"Not the police, you say?" Senor Hueso said as he started moving toward us menacingly. . . .

CHAPTER THREE

*T*HUD! Seconds later, we'd been tossed through a door into an alley. "Aw, man," Leo whined, "why can't anyone ever throw us into a nice soft pile of trash?"

I picked myself up with a groan. "Donnie, why didn't you just put a tracking device in the Turtle Tank? Once, you put a tracking device in a comic book!"

"A HIGHLY COLLECTIBLE comic book," Donnie corrected him. "I was getting around to putting a tracking device in the Turtle Tank." Then he remembered something. "But I DID install the shopping-cart protocol...."

Later we found out that right at that moment, Splinter was zooming down a wet street near the harbor, spraying water on people with the tank's tires. Suddenly, the front wheels locked! The tank slammed to a halt. Its back wheels popped up off the ground.

"What the . . . ?" Splinter said. "What happened?"

A robotic voice spoke from the Turtle Tank's speakers. "Shopping-cart protocol activated."

"What's that?"

"Similar to a high-tech shopping cart, I am programmed to stop if I go beyond a set perimeter."

"Shopping carts have technology?!"

A couple of minutes later, Splinter was hammering away with a wrench under the Turtle Tank's hood. He was trying to undo the shopping-cart protocol. Computer chips went flying.

"Useless," he growled. "Maybe I'll call April. She's no snitch."

A food truck pulled up next to the Turtle Tank. From inside the dark truck, the driver asked, "Need a hand, mate?" He had a strong English accent.

The driver got out of the food truck. It was Meat Sweats, the mutant pig chef guy from two stories ago! Unfortunately, when we'd tried to fill Splinter in on what a bad dude Meat Sweats was, he'd been too busy watching his favorite Japanese game show to pay attention. He had no idea he'd just been offered help by a guy who liked to drain the powers out of other mutants!

"GAH!" Splinter shouted when he saw Meat Sweats. "You're a freak of nature!"

"Sounds like the potbelly calling the kettle black," Meat Sweats observed coolly.

"Touché," Splinter said. "Gimme a ride uptown?" He slammed the hood closed. *WHUMP!* "I'll leave this here and hope it all works itself out."

Meat Sweats stroked his hairy chin. "I COULD do that. But how about we eat first? A drizzle of lemon over thinly sliced silverfish sashimi?"

Splinter looked impressed. "Fancy! I've only eaten silverfish off the bottom of my slipper!"

Smiling evilly, Meat Sweats put his hand on Splinter's back and ushered him into his food truck. "And I'll throw in a killer dessert!"

He licked his lips. . . .

CHAPTER FOUR

Jumping and flipping, we made our way across the city's rooftops. "Okay," Donnie said. "We'll find the Turtle Tank if we just follow the perimeter of the shopping-cart protocol's limit."

"There!" Mikey said, pointing down at the Turtle Tank parked in the street. It looked fantastic! It was totally tricked-out ⁺th armor, huge wheels, narrow windows ᶰot out of, and who knows how many hidden doohickeys! And the colors were rad: purple, blue, green, orange, and red. "Whoa!" we cried. "Donnie, nice work!"

"What's Dad doing down there?" Leo asked. Sure enough, Splinter was standing near the Turtle Tank.

Donnie scowled. "I should have KNOWN he took it! You can't trust adults! You leave the keys to your brainchild lying—"

Before Donnie could finish his rant, a large figure stepped out of the shadows and ushered Splinter into a food truck.

"Meat Sweats?!" I said. "What's HE doin' here? We gotta move, or Dad'll be toast!"

When I said that, I had no idea Meat Sweats was rubbing melted butter into Dad's fur, preparing him to be eaten! Dad was sitting on a folding chair inside the truck, scarfing down sushi, totally unaware that his life was in danger!

"This butter shampoo will make you feel . . . scrumptious!" Meat Sweats said, snickering. He picked up a big knife and started sharpening it. Dad just kept eating.

"I have a great idea for a chain of restaurants," Splinter said with his mouth full. "You're inside a giant wedge of cheese, and you eat your way out. I call it T.G.I. Parmesan. My sons think it's stupid."

"Sons?" Meat Sweats asked, puzzled. "What must they be? Chatty opossums?"

"No, no," Splinter said, shaking his head. "Turtles."

"Turtles?" Meat Sweats asked, remembering how we'd sent him packing, down in the subway tunnels. "Red, orange, blue, and purple?"

"Oh, you know their names!" Splinter said.

Meat Sweats looked out the truck's back window. "Yes, and they're right outside. Looking delicious!"

PTOOOF! Splinter spat out his food. "What?! We gotta bone out! My son can't find out I took his tank!" Determined to avoid getting in trouble with us, Splinter scrambled into the driver's seat and floored it. *VROOM!* Meat Sweats fell to the floor as the truck sped off, shocked by the old rat's energy. We jumped in the Turtle Tank and took off after them!

Dad raced through the city, skidding through his turns and driving over curbs. Meat Sweats got tossed around the back like popcorn in a pan.

"You took that tank from your own son?" Meat Sweats asked between tumbles.

"You're an animal!"

"I'm not taking the fall for this!" Splinter vowed.

"But what could your son do to you?"

"Purple's a monster!" Splinter cried. "He'll fry my TV so all I get is educational shows!"

CHAPTER
FIVE

Inside the Turtle Tank, Donnie stood with his back to the steering wheel, turning it with two of his battle shell's robotic arms while he proudly pointed out the tank's special features with his other arms. "Over there is navigation. Down here is a bowling-ball launcher. Strike! And there is the—"

"Soft-serve ice cream machine?" Mikey asked. "Tell me there's a sprinkles cannon!"

"Donnie, watch the road!" I told him.

"I wouldn't need to if you'd just take your seat," Donnie said.

"Uh, which one is mine?" I asked.

"It's the giant red one with your name and your exact lumbar settings!" Donnie said. "Just drive!"

I climbed into the big captain's seat. Pretty sweet.

We zoomed along the city streets, bouncing over potholes and careening around corners. Street lights and traffic lights flashed by the windows. Soon I caught up with Meat Sweats's food truck and pulled alongside. Donnie leaned out the passenger window. "I know you're in there!" he yelled to Splinter.

Dad dove under the dash, hiding. He hit the gas pedal with his hand to speed up. Meat Sweats jumped forward and grabbed the wheel. "What are you doing, you crazy old rat?!"

"You steer!" Splinter called up to him. "I'll pedal!"

The food truck roared through the night. I kept the Turtle Tank right next to 'em, mostly. We could hear Meat Sweats barking orders to Dad: "Slow! Fast! Brake, brake, BRAKE!" Leave it to Dad to scare a giant mutant with his driving!

Donnie hung out of the Turtle Tank's window again. "Dad!" he shouted. "I can see your tail! If you surrender now, there will be no consequences!"

Inside the food truck, Splinter hissed to Meat Sweats, "It's a lie! I taught him that one!" He reached up and yanked the steering wheel, slamming the food truck into the Turtle Tank. *WHAM!*

I leaned across to yell out the window at Dad. "You're with a very dangerous mutant, Pop! Meat Sweats just wants to eat you!"

Ignoring the threat, Splinter peered

up at the pig mutant. "Your name is Meat Sweats?"

"Actually, it's Rupert," Meat Sweats said. "Rupert Swaggart. You may remember me from my TV show."

"Was it one of those hilarious Japanese game shows where people got covered in baking soda and slid into a pool of vinegar?"

"Certainly not!"

"Then I'm gonna say it's doubtful I ever saw you," Splinter said. "Also, I'd go with Meat Sweats. It suits you. Rupert is more of a teddy bear's name."

Meat Sweats cranked the wheel, and the food truck flew around a turn.

"We gotta stop that truck!" I yelled.

Donnie grabbed a joystick. A target visor dropped over his eyes. "I'll blast it with the boom cannons!"

My first thought was *Boom cannons?*

That wasn't Donnie's best work. He needed to come up with a better name. My second thought was more important, but Leo beat me to it.

"But Dad's in that truck!" he shouted.

Donnie scowled. "You never let me shine." Then he brightened. "Harpoon hooks! With chains!"

CHAPTER SIX

***F**WOOM!*

Chains sprang from the Tank and hooked onto the roof of the truck.

Leo and Mikey jumped out and scurried across the links like tightrope walkers as the pavement raced beneath them. "Okay, Sweaty Spaghetti," Mikey shouted. "Give us our dad back!"

Splinter stayed under the dashboard, trying to hide. He looked up at Meat Sweats.

"Don't snitch me out, bro!" he pleaded.

"Yeah, hand over the fugitive!" Donnie called.

Meat Sweats kicked open the rear door of his truck. "I don't think so!" he growled. "You have a reservation in my stomach! Party of five, seating now!"

He hit a button, and the truck opened like a toolbox, forming a full kitchen! We saw cages full of mutants that Meat Sweats must have captured.

"Ooh," Mikey said when he saw the kitchen. "Is he finally gonna teach us how to make that pork risotto?"

Meat Sweats walked up to the mutants' cages. "Since I assume you won't go down without a fight, allow me to choose my weapon." He stopped by the cage of a mutant snake, reached through the bars, and grabbed the snake. Its energy flowed into him.

"He's getting the mutant snake's power!" Leo said.

Then something super disgusting happened. Meat Sweats hawked up a gob and spat it at us!

"Duck!" I warned. "It's a spitting cobra!"

When the venom hit the Turtle Tank, it rocked the tank, smoking as it burned the solid metal. "Donnie!" I cried. "What else have you got in this thing?"

"Ooh," Donnie said. "I've been wanting to try this!" He hit a button, launching a bowling ball.

"ARRGGH!" Meat Sweats grunted as it smacked him right in the face.

Dad floored it, and the truck went even faster as Meat Sweats spit venom at us from the back. But our chains were still hooked onto the truck, so we were towed behind it! Leo and Mikey kept making their way across the chains to the truck as it sped along.

But Meat Sweats was still spitting venom, melting the chains! He launched another gob of mutant snake poison at us . . .

. . . but Leo's glowing *odachi* sword created a portal in front of the gob! It flew into the portal, then exited another portal, heading straight for Meat Sweats!

The pig mutant faced the gob. "Oopsie . . ."

SPLAT!

The venom hit Meat Sweats right in the face! "GAAAAH!"

"Let's get him!" I cried.

But at that very moment, Meat Sweats whipped out his keys and hit a button on a remote control. All the cages opened and the mutants rushed out onto the road.

I hit the breaks, which snapped the chains and dropped Leo and Mikey to the street. Meat Sweats jumped into the driver's seat, threw Splinter out, and sped off!

Splinter ran after the truck. "Wait! Don't leave me!"

Leo, Mikey, and I laughed as Donnie sprinted after Dad, yelling, "You! You reckless, irresponsible ... You're watching the Book Report channel for a month!"